The Many Troubles
of
Andy
Russell

The Many Troubles
of
Andy
Russell

David A. Adler

With illustrations by
Will Hillenbrand

Gulliver Books
Harcourt Brace & Company
San Diego   New York   London

Thank you, Liz Van Doren,
for being my writing teacher,
editor, and friend.

—D. A. A.

Text copyright © 1998 by David A. Adler
Illustrations copyright © 1998 by Will Hillenbrand

Gulliver Books is a registered trademark of Harcourt Brace & Company.

Library of Congress Cataloging-in-Publication Data
Adler, David A.
The many troubles of Andy Russell/David A. Adler; with
illustrations by Will Hillenbrand.
p.   cm.
"Gulliver Books."
Summary: When some of his gerbils escape and he gets in trouble
for not paying attention in class, fourth-grader Andy Russell
worries about asking if a friend can move in with his family—
especially when he learns that his mother is going to have another baby.
ISBN 0-15-201900-6
[1. Family life—Fiction.   2. Friendship—Fiction.   3. Gerbils—
Fiction.   4. Worry—Fiction.]   I. Hillenbrand, Will, ill.
II. Title.
PZ7.A2615Man   1998
[Fic]—dc21   98-10788

Text set in Century Old Style
Designed by Kaelin Chappell

C E F D
Printed in the United States of America

Also by David A. Adler

Andy and Tamika

**School Trouble
for Andy Russell**

For my son, Eddie,
and for his cousins, Shira and Dahlia

—D. A. A.

Contents

Chapter 1
Gerbils on the Loose

Andy Russell rushed to the edge of the stairs and looked up. The doors to his parents' and sister Rachel's rooms were closed. He hurried back to the kitchen and climbed onto the counter by the sink. He reached up and pressed one hand to the ceiling to keep his balance.

Andy stretched. He was just able to touch the stack of plastic bowls on the top shelf of the cabinet, but he couldn't grab them.

I've got to stand on something else, Andy

thought. He looked down at the kitchen chairs. *Too high. If I put one on the counter and then stand on it, my head will hit the ceiling.* Andy looked at the shelf that held recipe cards and telephone books. *That's it,* he thought. *The Yellow Pages.*

Andy jumped from the counter. He opened the book to the back—1,288 pages. *That should do it.* Andy put it on the counter and climbed up.

He heard footsteps. He had to hurry. Someone was coming downstairs.

Andy pressed his hand against the ceiling again. He leaned forward and reached into the cabinet, but he still couldn't grab the bowls. He leaned forward a little more. Just as he got hold of the stack of bowls, his foot slipped and ripped the cover off the *Yellow Pages.* Andy fell into the sink. He knocked over a pot filled with soapy water and the bowls dropped from his hand to the floor.

The footsteps were getting closer.

Andy reached for the faucet to pull himself out of the sink, but his wet, soapy hand slipped and turned on the water. The water soaked the bottom of his pants legs and spilled on the floor.

"What happened? Are you hurt?" Mr. Russell

asked as he rushed into the kitchen and shut off the water.

"I'm just wet," Andy answered.

"Your foot is in the vegetable pot!" Mr. Russell said, and pulled a string bean off Andy's sneaker. "And your pants are all wet."

Andy held out his hand, and his father helped him out of the sink. "I was afraid Mom was coming down the stairs. I'm glad it was you."

"You didn't answer me. What happened? What were you doing in the sink? And take off those wet sneakers."

Andy took off his sneakers and socks. He collected the bowls while his father wiped the floor and counter with paper towels.

"Roll up the bottoms of your pants," Mr. Russell said. "They're dripping on the floor."

Andy rolled up his pants.

Mr. Russell wiped the floor again and asked, "Well, what were you doing in the sink?"

"I was getting bowls for the gerbils," Andy answered, "and I wouldn't have fallen into the sink and made such a mess if Mom didn't keep the bowls on the top shelf. Why does she do that?"

Andy looked up. His handprint was on the ceiling. All five fingers were nice and clear. He hoped his father wouldn't see it.

"Don't blame your mother for this mess," Mr. Russell said as he put the *Yellow Pages* back on the shelf. "She didn't fall in the sink. You did!"

Mr. Russell turned and looked at his son. "What happened to the bowls we bought at the pet shop?"

"They're still in the gerbil tanks, but believe me, Dad. We need more."

Mr. Russell refilled the vegetable pot with water and soap, and asked, "Why do we need more bowls?"

Just then Andy's older sister, Rachel, walked into the kitchen and said, "Hi, Monkey Face."

Rachel put a slice of bread into the toaster oven. She set the timer to two minutes and made sure to turn it and the toaster oven on at exactly the same moment.

Rachel ate the same breakfast every morning. "At two minutes, the toast is golden brown," she had once explained to her mother. "Anything more and it's too dark. Anything less and it's too bready."

"*Bready* is not a word," Mrs. Russell had told Rachel.

After two minutes, Rachel would put on a slice of American cheese and wait exactly one minute more, "So the cheese is just the right combination of soft and cheesy," Rachel had told her mother. "And *cheesy* IS a word!"

While Rachel stood by the toaster oven, she pointed at Andy's feet, held her nose, and said, "Wrap those in something. You're polluting the environment."

Andy made a face, pointed at his sister, and then spun one finger beside his head to indicate he thought she was crazy.

Rachel stuck out her tongue.

Then Andy whispered to his father, "Dad, come with me. I have to tell you something."

Andy took his socks and sneakers and led his father into the dining room.

"What is it?" Mr. Russell asked.

"It's trouble," Andy whispered. "Gerbil trouble. But I don't want Mom or Rachel to know about it. Please, promise you won't tell them."

Andy waited. His father didn't promise, but Andy was sure he would keep his secret. He was sure his dad wouldn't want Mrs. Russell or Rachel to know what he was about to tell him.

"I need the extra bowls"—Andy took a deep breath—"because I have to leave food in the basement and the hall because that's where some of them are."

"What!" Mr. Russell shouted.

"Sh!" Andy whispered.

He tiptoed to the doorway to see if Rachel had heard his father scream. She had one hand ready to open the toaster-oven door. She was watching the timer. Andy tiptoed back to his father. He was still holding his socks and sneakers.

"The gerbils in the middle tank got out," Andy whispered, "and I don't know how that happened unless, maybe, they watched me open and close it so often that they learned how to do it themselves. If I don't leave food for them, they might starve."

Andy suspected he hadn't completely closed the screen on top of the gerbils' tank, and he was sure his father suspected the very same thing. He was just glad his father didn't seem really angry.

"How many gerbils are out?" Mr. Russell asked.

"Well," Andy replied, "I think maybe seven. But don't worry. I'll take care of them. They're mostly in the basement, but I saw one in the upstairs hall, so that's where I'm leaving the food."

As Mr. Russell hurried to the basement, he told Andy, "I'm not worried about the gerbils. I'm worried about the house and your mother. She hasn't been feeling well, and I'm sure something like this would really upset her."

Andy was also sure it would upset her. His mother didn't like animals. She only agreed to let Andy have pets when he assured her she wouldn't have to take care of them, and if she didn't go into the basement, she wouldn't even see them.

Mr. Russell opened the door to the basement. He and Andy went in. Then Mr. Russell quickly closed the door.

From the top of the stairs, Andy looked around the large room. Along the wall with the staircase was a row of low bookcases, each with three shelves filled with books, toys, and the blocks Andy played with when he was much younger. On top of the bookcases were four tanks, three for his gerbils and one for his pet snake, Slither. Along the next wall hung framed family photographs. In front of the remaining two walls were a couch, a small table, and chairs.

Ta. Ta. Ta. . . . Ta. Ta. Ta.

"I think there's one under the couch," Andy said.

"Catch it! Catch it!" Mr. Russell told him.

They quickly ran down the steps. Mr. Russell lifted the front end of the couch. It was heavy. Inside, it had a hidden bed.

The gerbil looked up at Mr. Russell.

Andy gently put down his socks and sneakers. He walked very slowly toward the gerbil. "Don't be afraid," Andy said softly.

"I'm *not* afraid," Mr. Russell told him. "I'm upset, and I can't hold this up much longer."

"Dad, I was talking to the gerbil."

Andy moved slowly. "Don't be afraid," he said again. "I'm going to put you back in your home, where there's plenty of food and water and toys. I'm your friend, so don't be afraid."

"Don't sweet-talk him," Mr. Russell said. "Just catch him! Catch him!"

Andy reached for the gerbil's tail, but before he could catch it, the gerbil ran behind the bookcase. Mr. Russell slowly lowered the couch, and when it was just a few inches above the floor, he let it drop.

Bam.

Suddenly the basement door opened and Mrs. Russell looked in. "What are you doing down there? This is a school day. The bus will be here soon."

Mrs. Russell looked at Andy. She shook her head slightly and added, "Roll down your pants legs and put on your socks and sneakers."

"Yes, Mom."

"Please close the door," Mr. Russell said.

"Whatever you're doing down there, do it fast," Mrs. Russell told him. "Andy can't miss the bus, and Charles, you can't be late for work, especially not now." Then she closed the door.

"Why can't you be late for work, Dad?"

"Let's just catch the gerbils," Mr. Russell answered. It was clear to Andy that his father didn't want to say why he had to be on time. *Maybe Dad's in trouble at work,* Andy thought. *Maybe he messed up.*

"I'll catch them all, Dad. I promise."

Ta. Ta. Ta. . . . Ta. Ta. Ta.

A gerbil was running under the baseboard

heater. Andy reached for its tail, but the gerbil ran behind a bookcase and Andy couldn't get it.

"Dad, please, don't tell Mom they got out. She doesn't like my pets, and if she finds out the gerbils are loose, she won't, well, she won't be happy."

An odd look came over Mr. Russell's face and then the hint of a smile. He spoke slowly. "Gerbils on the loose will upset Mom, and we don't want that. If Mom doesn't ask me about them, I won't mention it."

Crash!

A gerbil had knocked over an open box of plastic stacking clowns and spilled them across the basement floor. Andy lunged after the gerbil and landed on the clowns. "Ouch!" Andy exclaimed as he reached under his stomach, pulled out a clown, and tossed it into the box. Then he sat up and put the other clowns in the box, too.

"Don't worry so much about me telling Mom," Mr. Russell said. "Worry about the gerbils. If they're not careful and keep knocking things over, I won't have to tell her they're loose. She'll find out on her own."

Chapter 2
Slither the Snake

Before Andy and his father went upstairs, they checked the screen tops of the two other gerbil tanks. The gerbils were inside, playing on the exercise wheels, crawling through the tunnels, and chewing the colored construction paper Andy had left for them the night before. The gerbils had chewed most of the paper into tiny pieces.

"They're busy making confetti," Andy told his father.

Andy sometimes called the gerbil tanks "confetti factories." The shelves of his closet were filled with bags of gerbil-made confetti. Andy was saving them to sell for New Year's Eve.

Mr. Russell was proud of Andy's confetti project. He said it showed Andy had a "real head for business," that when he finished school he would be able to take care of himself. Mrs. Russell wasn't impressed. She said, "If I find one scrap of gerbil-chewed paper upstairs, those animals go back to the pet shop!"

Next, Andy and his father looked in Slither's tank. The snake was Andy's reward for six "Be Good" weeks at the end of third grade, when he had paid attention in class and didn't argue with his teacher, Mr. Hoover. Andy had hoped to get a poisonous cobra or a squeezing python, but his parents refused to buy a dangerous snake and bought Slither instead, a nonpoisonous, nonsqueezing garter snake.

Slither ate minnows. Andy liked to watch the small bulge move down Slither's skinny body as he slowly digested each fish.

A few days after Andy got the snake, Slither escaped and was gone for three weeks. Mr.

Russell was sure he had slithered out of the house. He felt bad for Andy and bought two gerbils to take the snake's place. Andy put them in Slither's tank.

Mr. Russell had asked Jeff at the pet shop for male gerbils. It was clear a few weeks later, when Andy discovered one of the gerbils nursing seven babies, that Jeff had made a mistake. A while later she had babies again. Later the babies had babies.

And Slither hadn't slithered out of the house.

A few days after Andy got the gerbils, it rained. Rachel put her foot in her left rain boot and screamed.

She had found Slither.

Andy thanked Rachel for finding his snake, but she was screaming too loud to hear him. Rachel hated Andy's pets, perhaps even more than their mother did.

By this time the gerbils were living in Slither's tank, so Andy emptied an apple-juice jar, then put in some dirt, leaves, and Slither. Andy's father poked a few small holes in the top of the jar so the snake could breathe. That afternoon Mr. Russell bought a new tank with a screen on top.

Andy smiled now as he looked at Slither. The snake turned his head toward Andy. Slither stuck out his forked tongue. The tongue darted in and out a few times.

Andy said, "Good morning, Slither," and stuck out *his* tongue.

Andy checked his socks and sneakers. They were still wet. He hid them behind a chair and followed his father upstairs. Rachel was standing by the front door. "You'd better hurry," she told Andy as she left the house.

Andy ran upstairs, rolled down his pants legs, got dry socks, and put them on. Then he put on his dry winter boots. He ate a quick breakfast—a granola bar and chocolate milk.

Mrs. Russell stood by the door and watched Andy put on his jacket, take his backpack and lunch bag, and open the front door. Before she could ask him why he was wearing boots in the fall, Andy told his mother, "You look lovely this morning."

"Thank you," Mrs. Russell said as she went to the closet to get her own coat.

Andy was proud of himself. He had distracted his mother and said just the right thing. He thought that now, if she saw a gerbil on the couch, she might remember that he had said she looked lovely and not get so angry.

Andy ran to the bus stop and waited there with Rachel and the Belmont girls. He looked at Rachel and remembered when she had found Slither. She had run upstairs, changed her socks, washed her feet, and screamed again and again about "that slimy, stinky thing."

"Snakes don't stink!" Andy had told Rachel as he gently took Slither out of her boot.

Andy smiled as he wondered what Rachel would do if she found gerbils in her boots. She'd probably scream so loud she would get laryngitis. Then she wouldn't be able to talk. *A quiet Rachel!* Andy thought that would be great.

Andy's parents drove past the bus stop. Mrs. Russell was driving. First she would leave Mr. Russell off at the library, where he was helping to build an extension to the reading room. He was a carpenter and was doing some of the woodwork. Then Mrs. Russell would go to the high school, where she taught mathematics.

Just as Andy saw the bus approaching, he realized he had forgotten to leave out the bowls of food. The house was locked and his parents were gone. Rachel had a key, but to get it, he would have to tell her about the gerbils. And, even with the key, if he ran home, he would miss the bus and have no way to get to school. Andy realized there was nothing he could do. He had real trouble this morning. He hoped the gerbils wouldn't be hungry and that he could catch them all before his mother or Rachel discovered they were out.

The bus stopped and the door opened. Rachel and the Belmonts got on, and just as Andy put his right foot on the first step, Tamika Anderson shouted, "Wait! Wait for me!"

Andy waited for Tamika with his right foot on the first step of the bus and his left foot on the curb.

"You can get on. I'll wait for her," Mr. Cole, the bus driver, said. "Don't I always wait for her?"

It was true. Tamika was late for the bus almost every morning, and when she yelled, "Wait!" Mr. Cole always did.

Andy got on the bus and said hello to his friend Bruce, who was sitting near Mr. Cole.

Bruce put one hand on his head and the other beneath his chin. Then he waved both hands. A long time ago, when they had first met at school, Andy had made that their secret wave. But now he wished Bruce would not do that every morning. He thought a secret wave was kindergarten stuff.

There were no empty seats near Bruce. Andy found one in the back, right behind Rachel. Tamika followed him onto the bus. Her sneakers were untied and her shirtsleeves were unbuttoned.

"I'm sorry I made you wait," she told Mr. Cole. She stood for a moment just inside the bus, trying to catch her breath.

"That's OK," the bus driver said as he pulled the lever to close the door. "I'm used to it."

Tamika walked down the narrow aisle and took the seat across from Andy.

"Hi," Andy said.

"Hi," Tamika replied. "I was helping Mrs. Perlman wash the breakfast dishes. That's why I'm late."

Andy held Tamika's backpack while she tied her shoes and buttoned her shirtsleeves. She took a mirror from her pack and looked into it.

"Yuck!" she said. "My hair ribbons don't match my shirt."

"And your socks don't match each other," Andy said as he returned her backpack. "One's red and the other is brown."

"I'll get up earlier tomorrow. I will."

"Maybe," Andy said. "Or maybe you'll be late again and say what you always say, that you'll get up earlier tomorrow."

Tamika took a deep breath and then asked, "Did you talk to your parents yet?"

Andy shook his head and pointed to Rachel. Tamika didn't understand.

Andy took out his homework pad. He opened to a blank page and wrote, I DIDN'T ASK MY PARENTS YET AND RACHEL DOESN'T KNOW ABOUT IT!

"We can tell Ra—," Tamika started to say, but Andy put his finger to his lips and gave Tamika the homework pad. Tamika wrote, WE CAN TELL RACHEL. SHE'S MY FRIEND, TOO.

Andy took back the pad and read Tamika's message. Then he shook his head and wrote, I'LL TAKE CARE OF THIS.

He gave Tamika the pad. She turned to the

previous page and asked, "Did we have any history homework?"

"We had to review chapter seven."

"We did?" Tamika asked. She looked out the bus window. "We're at Hamilton Avenue. I have time," she said, and took out her history book.

When they arrived at school, the yard was already clear. Tamika and Andy were the last off the bus. They hurried into the building.

All during class Andy looked right at Ms. Roman, his fourth-grade teacher. He didn't want her to think he wasn't listening. Then she might write another note to his parents. But he *wasn't* listening. He was thinking about the gerbils, wondering if they were still in the basement, if they were hungry, and if his mother would go home for lunch and find them. Andy imagined the gerbils outside their tank, looking in, seeing the food, water, toys, and paper, and feeling sorry they had left their comfortable home. He was also thinking about his secret with Tamika.

"Andrew, are you paying attention?" Ms. Roman asked.

Andrew was Andy's real name. But only Ms. Roman called him that.

Andy considered changing the subject by telling Ms. Roman she looked lovely. But then he looked at her big gray tent dress and brown work shoes, and decided that even Ms. Roman wouldn't believe she looked good.

"Andrew, are you paying attention?" Ms. Roman asked again.

Andy smiled. "Yes, Ms. Roman."

"Then what's the answer?"

The answer? What was the question?

Andy looked at Tamika, and she shook her head. She hadn't been listening, either.

Andy looked next at his friend Bruce. He was busy scribbling in his notebook. Andy thought Bruce was probably writing another silly poem.

Ms. Roman was standing next to the globe. Perhaps she had asked Andy a geography question. He remembered that China is the name of a country where a lot of people live and that dishes are made of it, and he thought it could be the answer to lots of questions.

"China," Andy said.

"China! What sort of an answer is that? We're doing math!"

A few of Andy's classmates laughed. Many of

the others looked up. It was clear to Andy that they weren't paying attention, either. They hadn't heard Ms. Roman's question nor Andy's ridiculous answer.

Ms. Roman called on Stacy Ann Jackson. Stacy Ann sat right in front of Andy.

"Four hundred and twelve," Stacy Ann said in her best I-know-and-you-don't tone.

"That's right."

"Thank you," Stacy Ann said sweetly to Ms. Roman. Then, when Ms. Roman turned to the chalkboard, Stacy Ann whispered to Andy, "*I* was listening."

Andy hated Stacy Ann Jackson. She was so phony. He couldn't understand why Ms. Roman and all the other teachers liked her.

Andy tried to pay attention to the rest of the math lesson, but it was a real struggle. He kept thinking about the gerbils and his secret with Tamika. Andy was relieved when the bell rang and it was time for lunch.

In the cafeteria, Andy, Tamika, and Bruce sat far away from most of their classmates. Andy was about to tell Tamika and Bruce about the gerbils when Bruce took a paper from his shirt pocket

and asked, "Do you want to hear the poem I wrote during math?"

"No."

Bruce read it anyway.

> *"A crocodile bath*
> *or doing math.*
> *Which is worse?*
> *Ask the nurse."*

"Very nice," Andy said. "Now eat your lunch."

"I'm calling this poem 'Crocodile Math,' and I'm going to submit it to the school newspaper or maybe to a magazine."

"Why would you ask a nurse about a crocodile or math?" Tamika asked. "She knows about Band-Aids and thermometers, not reptiles and numbers."

"I was using my creative license," Bruce answered as he carefully folded the paper and returned it to his shirt pocket. "My dad says I'm creative, and creative people make a difference. We change the world."

Andy said, "I hope creative people change their underwear, too."

"What!"

"Just kidding! Eat your lunch," Andy said again, "so I can tell you about my gerbil troubles."

Bruce opened his lunch bag and unwrapped the aluminum foil from his sandwich. He lifted the corner of the top slice of bread and said, "Cream cheese again! I get the same boring lunch every day."

Andy gave his sandwich to Bruce.

Bruce inspected Andy's sandwich and said, "Ah, peanut butter."

Bruce offered to trade Andy his cream-cheese sandwich, but Andy didn't want it. "I can't eat. I have too many troubles."

Andy gave Bruce his apple and cupcake, too. He opened his container of chocolate milk, pushed in a straw, and drank slowly.

"Hey, thanks," Bruce said.

He took the tops off the two sandwiches and turned the two slices of bread and cream cheese over, placing them on top of the two halves of Andy's sandwich. "Now I have two cream-cheese-and-peanut-butter sandwiches."

Bruce remade the sandwiches. After he bit into one, Tamika said, "You didn't have to put them together. If you ate them separately, you would have been eating the same thing. Everything just gets mixed up in your stomach anyway."

"Ig taks etter is ay," Bruce said with his mouth full of cream cheese, peanut butter, and bread. He swallowed and said again, "It tastes better this way."

"Oh, stop talking about food. I have real important stuff to tell you," Andy said. "But not here. Outside."

"As soon as I finish," Bruce said.

Tamika ate her lunch quickly, threw out her empty bag, and waited with Andy while Bruce ate the sandwiches, an orange, and Andy's apple and cupcake. He drank two containers of apple juice.

"Are you done?" Andy asked.

Bruce checked inside his lunch bag and Andy's to see if there was anything left. There wasn't.

"Done," he said. "Let's go outside."

Bruce dropped the aluminum foil, empty lunch bags, and drink containers in the large garbage can by the door. Then Andy led Tamika and Bruce outside.

"Hey, Tamika!" Rachel called. She was jumping

rope with a group of her friends. "Do you want to play?"

Tamika shook her head and pointed to Andy.

Andy led Tamika and Bruce to a corner of the playground and told them about the gerbils.

"So why is that such a big secret?" Bruce asked.

Andy pointed to Rachel. "We have to catch the gerbils before my mother or Rachel finds out. Will you help?"

"I really want to," Tamika said, "but I can't. I have to go to the dentist. The Perlmans want my teeth checked before they go to South America."

The Perlmans were Tamika's foster parents. She had been living with them for the past year, ever since Tamika's parents were badly hurt in a car accident. At first it was expected this arrangement would last just a few months, but the Andersons were still in a rehabilitation center, and now the Perlmans were preparing to go to South America for their work.

"I'll help," Bruce said. "It will be fun. We can pretend we're on a lion safari. No...no, a gerbil safari."

The bell rang. Lunch period was over. Bruce ran toward the door. Andy was about to follow him when Tamika grabbed his arm. "When will you ask your parents if I can move in?" Tamika asked. "Please, do you think you can ask them today?"

That was Andy's secret with Tamika. He had promised to ask his parents if she could stay with his family for the year the Perlmans would be in South America—or until her parents were better.

"I'll talk to them. I promise. And if they say yes, they'll speak to Rachel. They'll probably want you to stay in her room and, believe me, it's better for my parents to ask Rachel instead of you or me."

Tamika said, "Maybe you're right."

"But first," Andy told her, "I have to get all the gerbils. If Mom finds one upstairs, she might not even let *me* stay in the house."

After lunch Ms. Roman talked about the fourth-grade carnival. It would raise money for charity and would be in three weeks, on the Monday before Thanksgiving. She wanted everyone to think of fun booths and to look at home for books and toys they no longer wanted. They would use them as prizes. The money they raised would be for the local soup kitchen to help pay for their Thanksgiving dinner. Andy thought making a carnival would be exciting. But even though he tried to listen to the talk about the booths and the prizes, he kept thinking about the gerbils.

When the school bell rang, Ms. Roman looked out across the class, smiled, and said, "Well, that's it. You go home and do your homework, and I'll prepare tomorrow's lessons. Go on."

School was out.

Andy loaded his backpack. He didn't want to think about which books he needed for homework, so he took them all.

Stacy Ann Jackson turned.

She smiled.

Then she took a note from her pocket. FOR ANDY was written on the outside of it. It was from Bruce. Stacy read from the note. "Should I bring my butterfly net? It might help us catch the gerbils."

Stacy Ann wrinkled her nose. She bent her fingers so her hands looked like paws and held them near her face. "Did your gerbils get out?" she squeaked.

"That was *my* note," Andy said, and grabbed it.

Stacy Ann smiled. "It landed by my desk. I thought it was for me."

Stacy Ann picked up her books. "Rachel must love having wild, stupid rodents running through your house. It's almost as bad as having a wild, stupid brother."

Stacy Ann Jackson turned and left the room.

Andy grabbed his backpack and started to run after her, but he had grabbed his pack upside down and all his books and papers fell out.

"Tamika, Bruce!" Andy called. "Stop her! Stop Stacy Ann! Don't let her talk to Rachel."

Chapter 3
More Trouble

Tamika and Bruce ran out of the room.

Andy packed his backpack again and this time he closed the zipper. He hurried toward the door, but before he could leave the room, Ms. Roman stopped him.

"Andrew, I was disappointed this morning. You weren't paying attention to the math lesson."

Ms. Roman was sitting at her desk. The class record book was open.

"I can't really talk now," Andy said. "If I don't hurry outside, I'll miss my bus."

"Andrew, your mother teaches in the high school. I will see her at the district meeting next week and she'll ask me how you're doing. What should I tell her?"

"Please, tell her I'm trying. I'm doing my best. I'll pay attention tomorrow. I really will."

"I hope so," Ms. Roman said. "I really do."

Andy waited.

"That's it," Ms. Roman said. "Now you hurry to the bus."

Andy ran outside and found Tamika and Bruce standing right in front of Stacy Ann. When she moved one way, so did they. When she moved the other way, they did, too.

"Let me go," Stacy Ann shouted. "I'll miss my bus."

Andy looked at the buses waiting by the curb. Some already had their engines running. "Let her go," Andy said. He couldn't worry about Stacy Ann Jackson now. He was too upset by the prospect of Ms. Roman telling his mother that he answered "China" to a *math* problem. His mother taught math and thought it was *so* interesting.

Stacy Ann ran to her bus. It was the first in line. She got on just before the door closed. Andy, Tamika, and Bruce went to their bus.

Rachel was sitting right behind Mr. Cole. "Hi, Monkey Face," she said when Andy got on.

"Yeah, sure," he answered.

Andy, Tamika, and Bruce sat together on the last seat. "I told Stacy Ann her slip was showing," Tamika said. "That's how I got her to stop. Then she looked down and saw that she wasn't wearing a dress or slip. She was wearing pants. Isn't that great!"

Andy nodded.

Bruce said, "And I told her she had her socks on the wrong feet. You see, Stacy Ann is not always so smart. Sometimes *I'm* the smart one. It doesn't matter what foot you put your socks on."

Andy turned to Bruce and said, "Well, smart one, it was because of your note about the butterfly net that Stacy Ann knows about the gerbils. Writing that note and throwing it near her desk wasn't very smart. And, as if your note and the gerbils aren't enough trouble, Ms. Roman reminded me that she's going to see my mom at a meeting next week. If I don't start paying attention, I know she'll tell my mother."

Andy looked out the window and said softly, "And it's so hard to listen in her class."

The bus started to move. Andy turned from the window and was startled to see Bruce staring at him.

"I'm sorry about the note," Bruce said, "and I'm sorry about Ms. Roman." He waited a moment. Then he looked down at the floor of the bus and asked softly, "Can we still play gerbil safari?"

"Sure," Andy replied. "I'll give you a big hunter's gun that shoots tranquilizer pellets."

"Really?"

"Of course not. I'm just kidding."

"And Andy," Tamika said, "don't worry so much about Ms. Roman. When she meets your mother, she'll probably tell her something good."

"Yeah," Bruce said. "Sometimes I worry so much about something, then it never happens."

During the ride home, while Tamika and Bruce talked, Andy stared out the window. He knew Tamika and Bruce were probably right, but still, he worried.

Andy imagined Ms. Roman telling his mother, "Your son Andrew pays absolutely no attention in class. It's a wonder he learns anything! One day he'll wake up from whatever he dreams about and find the school day is over and everyone has gone home."

Why does Mom have to be a teacher? Andy asked himself. *Why can't she be a carpenter, like Dad. He never meets Ms. Roman at meetings.* Then Andy remembered the gerbils. He hoped his mother hadn't gone home for lunch and found them running around the house.

"Let's go! Let's go! It's our stop," Tamika said. She was shaking Andy.

Andy, Tamika, and Bruce ran down the center aisle of the bus and jumped down the two steps to the street.

"I'll see you tomorrow," Tamika said after they had crossed the street. "And please, ask your parents about me." She ran next door to the Perlmans'.

"What did she say about your parents?" Bruce asked.

Andy turned, looked at Bruce, and said, "I can't tell you right now."

"You're keeping a secret from me?" Bruce asked. "But I'm your best friend."

"I really can't tell you," Andy said again. "I really can't."

Andy walked ahead. When he reached his house, Rachel was already there, opening the front door. Andy pushed in ahead of her and said, "Bruce and I are working in the basement, so stay out!"

"Don't worry. You can go in that basement with the gerbils and snake. I do my homework in the kitchen."

Andy stuck out his tongue at Rachel. Bruce smiled. Then they both hurried to the basement and closed the door.

Bruce sat at the end of the couch, next to the small table with the telephone. He picked up the handset and punched in his number. When his mother answered, he said, "I'm at Andy's. Can I stay to play and do my homework?" He listened and said, "Thanks, Mom."

After Bruce hung up the telephone, he and Andy searched the basement for gerbils.

The box of plastic stacking clowns had been

turned over again. There was lots of chewed-up paper on the floor.

Ta. Ta. Ta.... Ta. Ta. Ta.

"Sh. There's one under the heater," Andy whispered.

Andy took off his backpack and walked slowly toward the baseboard heater. Bruce followed him.

A gerbil tail was sticking out from under the heater.

Andy reached for the gerbil, but it ran toward Bruce with its tail still sticking out. Bruce took out his pocket ruler and stuck it under the heater, blocking the way. The gerbil stopped, turned, and ran back to where Andy was waiting. He grabbed its tail, pulled the gerbil out, and as he carried it to the tank, he told the gerbil, "I was worried about you. I'm glad you didn't starve."

"That was great," Andy told Bruce. "You're the chaser. I'm the catcher. We're a team."

"Yeah," Bruce said. "You don't have to worry. We'll catch all the gerbils."

Andy and Bruce searched for more gerbils. When they didn't find any, Andy put his ear flat on the floor and listened for them.

"There's something under there," Andy said, and crawled to the big cloth-covered chair. He reached under it and took out an autograph book. Andy said, "It's Rachel's. She's been searching all over for this."

He flipped through the book. "The gerbils chewed some of the pages—through Donna's poem, Beth's rebuses, and Freddy's icky birthday note. Now I'm in more trouble."

He put the book in his back pocket.

Andy found gerbil teeth marks in the television wire, too, and in the bottom of the bookcase.

"Your gerbils are worse than termites," Bruce said. "They must be really hungry."

For the next hour, Andy and Bruce listened, searched for, and chased after gerbils. Andy caught one more by grabbing its tail and another by dropping a towel on top of it; he scooped up the towel and put the gerbil gently into the tank.

"Maybe that's all of them," Bruce said.

"No. There were at least seven."

Click.

Bruce said, "I think I hear something."

"Uh-oh. That's not a gerbil," Andy told him. He quietly climbed the basement stairs and pushed

open the door just a little. "It's my parents," Andy whispered. "They're home early."

Through the crack in the open door, Andy watched his mother come in first. She moved very slowly, hardly lifting her feet. Her coat was hanging open with the belt dragging on the floor. Mr. Russell was right behind her. He helped her into the house.

Andy whispered to Bruce, "They're home early. I wonder what's wrong." Andy watched his parents go upstairs and then said, "Mom looks sick."

Bruce said, "I bet your dad told her about the gerbils. That's why she's sick."

"Oh, I hope not," Andy said. "He promised he wouldn't."

Andy waited. He expected someone to scream for him to come upstairs. When no one did, he told Bruce, "I may as well get it over with."

Bruce said, "Don't worry. Your mom knows you're just a kid."

"I don't think that will help," Andy said. He took a deep breath and told Bruce, "You stay here and look for gerbils. I'll go upstairs so Mom can yell at me."

Chapter 4
The Secret

Andy wondered what his mother would say and what he could tell her. *I know,* he thought. *I'll tell her not to yell at me. She should yell at the gerbils. They're the ones running loose and leaving droppings all over the house.* Then Andy thought, *Maybe I shouldn't say anything about the droppings.*

Andy walked past the kitchen. Rachel was sitting at the table with her schoolbooks in a neat pile on her left and one book open in front of her. To her right was a glass of milk on a place mat along with a neatly folded napkin.

You're lucky, Andy thought. *You never get in trouble.*

Andy thought some more about what he could tell his mother. *I know. I'll promise to punish the gerbils. I'll take away their toys and when the TV is on, I'll cover their tank with a dark cloth so they can't watch.* Andy smiled. *That's pretty funny.*

Andy walked upstairs, to his parents' bedroom. Mrs. Russell was lying on the bed with her eyes closed. She was still dressed in her school clothes. Even her shoes were still on. Mr. Russell was sitting beside her, holding a large green basin.

"Hello, Mom."

Mrs. Russell opened her eyes. She slowly lifted her head and looked at Andy. Her eyes were red. Her lips were pale. Her skin was almost green.

"Mom, you look terrible."

Mrs. Russell put her head down.

"I'm sorry you feel so bad and I know it's my fault. But don't worry. Bruce and I caught three of them. I'll go right back down and catch the rest."

"That's nice," Mrs. Russell said with her head still on the pillow. "You have a nice catch with Bruce."

Mr. Russell put the basin down and got up from the bed. He took Andy's arm and led him out of the room. "Your mother is not feeling well," he whispered.

"It's your fault, Dad. You shouldn't have told her about the gerbils."

Mr. Russell put his finger to his lips and said, "Sh, she doesn't know about the gerbils and don't you tell her."

"Then why does she look like that? Is she sick?"

"No."

Andy looked in the room. Mrs. Russell was leaning over the basin.

"She sure *looks* sick," Andy said. "She's about to barf."

"Go into your room and wait there," Mr. Russell told him. "I'll get Rachel. I need to talk to both of you."

Andy wondered what his dad needed to talk about. *Maybe Mom had caught that "berry-berry" disease from the gerbils, or some rare Chinese virus. Maybe the house will be quarantined. That wouldn't be so bad. I'll probably learn more watching cartoons all day than listening to Ms. Roman.*

When Andy sat on the edge of his bed, he felt Rachel's autograph book in his pocket. He pushed the book in deeper, so it wouldn't stick out. Then he scooted back, stretching his legs out on top of the bed. If his mother could wear her shoes in bed, then so could he.

Bruce walked into the room. "Hey! Look what I caught!" He was holding a gerbil by its tail. The gerbil was wriggling, trying to get loose.

Andy jumped off his bed. "Get downstairs with that and don't let anyone see you. I don't need more trouble."

Andy peeked into the hall and saw his father and Rachel coming up the stairs. They stopped to look in on Mrs. Russell.

"No. Don't go to the basement. Hide."

"Where?" Bruce asked.

Andy looked around the room.

"In my closet. No. It's full of stuff. There's no room. Hide under the bed."

Bruce quickly crawled under the bed. Andy draped a blanket over the side and sat down.

"Quit wriggling," Bruce said.

Andy bent forward and told him, "I'm not wriggling."

"Not you. The gerbil. It's getting loose."

"Hey, Monkey Face," Rachel said as she walked in. She looked for someplace to sit. "What a mess," she said as she pushed books, papers, candy wrappers, and a pair of pajamas off Andy's desk chair and sat down.

Mr. Russell leaned against the edge of Andy's desk. He started to say something and then stopped.

"It's not my fault," Andy said quickly. "The man at the pet shop didn't say anything about a berry disease or a virus from gerbils."

Mr. Russell looked at his son. "Andy, what I'm about to tell you has nothing to do with gerbils."

"Then it's Ms. Roman," Andy said. "It's impossible to listen to her all the time. She's as boring as breadsticks."

"As boring as breadsticks?" Rachel asked. "What does that mean?"

"Stop it, both of you," Mr. Russell said. A strange look came over his face and then a faint smile. "I have something important and wonderful to tell you," he said, "but it's a secret, a good secret."

"A *good* secret?" Rachel asked.

"Did we win the lottery?" Andy asked.

"It's better than the lottery," Mr. Russell said. "It's the best secret there is."

Mr. Russell smiled again.

"Your mother isn't sick."

He paused.

"And she really doesn't want people at her school making a fuss, so she's not telling them yet."

He paused again.

"And we're only telling you because we don't want you to think Mom is sick, and we need you to be helpful."

"Telling us what?" Andy shouted. "So far you haven't told us anything!"

"It's loose," Bruce said.

Andy coughed and kicked the side of his bed.

"What's that? Did you say something?" Mr. Russell asked.

Andy hit his chest and coughed again.

"No. I didn't say anything."

"Well," Mr. Russell went on, "don't tell this to anyone, not even any of your closest friends."

Andy's bed moved.

Andy looked down. A gerbil tail was sticking out from underneath the bed. Then the gerbil turned and it was looking up, right at Andy.

Andy glanced at his father, then at Rachel. Neither of them had noticed the gerbil. With hand signals, Andy told the gerbil to go under the bed. The gerbil tilted its head slightly. It didn't seem to understand.

"I know Mom doesn't look well now," Mr. Russell said. "That's because she has morning sickness. It's not serious. Women often get it during the first few months of pregnancy."

Mr. Russell looked at Andy and Rachel and smiled. "That's right. Mom is pregnant. We're going to have a baby."

Chapter 5
Get It Away

Andy looked away from the gerbil to his father. Mr. Russell was smiling broadly.

"Really?" Rachel asked.

Mr. Russell nodded.

"Oh, this is so exciting!" Rachel exclaimed.

"Mom better be careful," Andy warned. "With all that barfing, she might barf up the baby."

"Oh, Andy," Rachel said, "you can't barf a baby." Then she turned to her father and asked, "Do you know if it's a girl or a boy? Janet's mother had a baby and they knew it was going to be a girl. There's a test she took to find out."

"I hope it's a boy," Andy said.

"Well," Rachel said, "I hope it's a girl."

"Isn't this great news?" Mr. Russell asked. "Isn't this great?"

The bed moved. A hand shot out toward the gerbil but missed. The gerbil ran across the room, right in front of Rachel.

"Help! A mouse!" Rachel shouted. She quickly lifted her feet off the floor and then climbed onto Andy's desk, right on top of his pencils, markers, dinosaur collector cards, and used tissues.

The gerbil ran under the desk and into a corner of the room. Andy lay down on the floor and spread out his arms. The gerbil turned to one side and saw Andy's right hand waiting. It turned to the other side and saw Andy's left hand.

"Don't be afraid, little friend," Andy said. "I won't hurt you."

Andy moved closer, and as he did the gerbil looked straight at Andy and in a panic tried to run under him, but instead it ran right into Andy's shirt pocket. Andy got up, pulled the

gerbil out by its tail, held it in front of Rachel, and said, "This isn't a mouse. It's a gerbil."

Rachel waved her arms and shouted, "Get it away from me! Get it away!"

Bruce stuck his head out from under the bed and said, "Don't be afraid. Gerbils are really very friendly."

"Hey!" Rachel shouted. "Where did you come from?"

"I came from school," Bruce said as he slowly crawled out. "You saw me on the bus, remember? I'm helping Andy catch the gerbils."

"Ger*bils!*" Rachel said. "You mean there are more of them running around this house? Oh, you just wait. You just wait." She got off the desk. A tissue was stuck to the seat of her leggings. "Yuck," she said, and brushed it off. "Just wait until I tell Mom. She'll make you get rid of all of them and that snake, too, and then she'll really punish you."

Rachel took a step toward the door, but Mr. Russell stood in her way.

"You're not telling your mother anything about this. She already feels nauseous and this will only make her feel worse."

Rachel folded her arms and said, "Then you'll punish Andy and you'll get rid of his animals."

"No one is punishing Andy. His gerbils got loose and he's catching them. You can either help Andy and Bruce catch the gerbils or you can help me take care of your mother."

"That's what always happens around here. Andy gets away with everything," Rachel muttered. "I'll help you, Dad. I'll take care of Mom. I'd rather hold a barf basin than chase after mice."

"They're gerbils," Andy said.

"Whatever."

"And Bruce," Mr. Russell said, "what you heard in this room about a baby is a Russell family secret. Don't tell anyone."

"Don't worry," Bruce said, "I can keep a secret."

"Good," Mr. Russell said.

Andy was still holding on to the gerbil. "Here, hold him," Andy told Bruce. "I'll get something to put him in."

He turned and gave Bruce the gerbil.

"Hey," Rachel said. "Is that my autograph book in your back pocket?"

"Oh, yes," Andy said, and gave it to her. "I found it. Aren't you glad?"

Rachel opened the book and asked, "Did you tear these pages?"

Andy shook his head and mumbled, "The gerbils chewed on them."

"This is too much. This is just too much," Rachel said.

Then there was a faint call from Andy's parents' bedroom. "Charles, Charles, I need you."

"Rachel, come with me," Mr. Russell said as he turned to leave, "and don't you say a word about the gerbils."

"I'll try not to say anything," Rachel said, "but it won't be easy."

After Mr. Russell and Rachel left the room, Andy opened the closet door and took out an empty shoe box. He punched a few holes in the cover. Bruce put the gerbil in the box and Andy quickly put the top on.

Bruce said, "You're lucky your mother is pregnant. If she wasn't, Rachel would have told her about the gerbils and you would get in *real* trouble."

"I'm lucky," Andy said, "because I might get a brother."

Bruce smiled and said, "Adults get funny when they have a baby. I know my parents did when Danny was born. They made everyone be really quiet and they washed their hands a lot and every time Danny did something, they made a fuss like he was some kind of genius. They kept telling me to whisper, like Danny might listen to what I was saying."

"Bruce, they told you to whisper because they didn't want you to wake him."

"Oh."

Bruce kept talking about Danny, but Andy was no longer paying attention. He was thinking about having a baby in the house, having to whisper all the time, and that awful baby smell that Danny had.

He also thought about Tamika. Andy had hoped Tamika could live with them. But Bruce was right—adults *do* get funny when they have a baby. This was probably the very worst time to ask if Tamika could move in.

"And listen to this!" Bruce said.

Andy looked at his friend.

"I once changed Danny's yucky diaper and he squirted all over me. I had to change my shirt and everything."

"That's nice," Andy said.

"No, it's not," Bruce responded. "It's disgusting."

"Right, it's disgusting," Andy said, and held up the shoe box. "Let's put this gerbil in the tank with its friends and catch the others."

Chapter 6
The Trap

When they passed the door to Andy's parents' bedroom, Bruce smiled and said, "I hope you feel better, Mrs. Russell."

Andy looked in the room. Mr. Russell was standing by the window. He turned and looked at Bruce. Rachel was sitting on the floor, near the bed, holding the green basin. She looked up. Mrs. Russell looked, too, and gave Andy and Bruce a weak smile.

She doesn't look pregnant, Andy thought. *She*

just looks nauseous. Andy pulled on the back of Bruce's shirt and whispered, "Let's go."

"You may have the flu," Bruce continued. "My mother had it last year and for a few days she felt really bad."

Andy grabbed Bruce's arm and pulled him away from the door.

"What were you doing?" Andy asked when they were downstairs.

Bruce said, "I know about old people. They like it when you ask about their health."

Andy opened the basement door, pulled Bruce along, quickly closed the door behind them, and said, "You know my mother doesn't have the flu. She's pregnant."

"Now your mother thinks I don't know the Russell family secret. That's why I said that."

Andy just shook his head and walked down the basement steps. He opened the closet door, took out a flashlight, and turned it on. Then he crawled on the floor and pointed the light under the baseboard heater.

"I know the gerbils were here. They left droppings."

Andy crawled to the couch and looked under

there, too. Then he looked among the toys and books.

Ta. Ta. Ta.

"Did you hear that?" Andy whispered.

Bruce nodded.

"Where did it come from?"

Bruce pointed to the bookcase. "Behind there," I think.

Andy got on a chair and moved aside books and toys that were on top of the bookcase. Using the beam from the flashlight, he tried to look behind it, but he couldn't see anything. Andy got off the chair, returned it to its place by the table, went to the storage room, and came out with a ladder. He climbed the ladder and tried again to look behind the bookcase.

"I still can't see anything."

"I know," Bruce said, "but even if you saw one back there, how would you get it?"

Andy came down the ladder and sat on its bottom rung. He shook his head and said, "They're smaller than we are, but we should be smarter. There must be some way to catch the gerbils."

Bruce said, "Of course we're smarter than gerbils. We're in the fourth grade."

Bruce smiled. Then he said, "And don't worry. We'll catch all the gerbils."

"Thanks."

Andy sat on the bottom rung of the ladder for a while and thought. Then he went over to the two full gerbil tanks and looked in. Gerbils were playing on the exercise wheel and others were crawling through the long, twisted plastic tunnel to get to the food bowl.

"That's it!" Andy said, and clapped his hands. "We *won't* catch the gerbils. We'll outsmart them."

Andy returned the ladder to the storage room. Then he went upstairs. He looked into his parents' bedroom. Mr. Russell was patting Mrs. Russell's back while she leaned over the green basin. Rachel was holding the basin with one hand. She held her nose with her other hand, and her eyes were closed.

Andy went quickly to his room and emptied the wastebasket onto the floor. He kicked the trash under his bed, took the wastebasket to the basement, set it on the table, and filled it with gerbil food.

Andy put his face in the wastebasket and took a deep breath.

"Aah," Andy said. "The gerbils will smell that and say, 'Food! Let me get some.' This wastebasket is real deep. Once they get in, they won't be able to climb out."

Bruce asked, "But how will they get in?"

"Just watch."

Andy pulled back the screen from the top of one of the tanks. He took out the twisted plastic tunnel and then very carefully put the screen back on. He took the tunnels from the other tanks, too, and put them all on the floor.

"Can you help me take these apart?"

"Sure," Bruce said, "but why?"

"You'll see."

Andy and Bruce pulled and turned the plastic tubes until they had separated them all. Then they put the pieces together into one very long tunnel. Andy set one end over the wastebasket and the other on the floor. The tunnel was now one very long covered ramp leading to the food.

"What do we do now?" Bruce asked.

"We just wait," Andy told him. "The gerbils

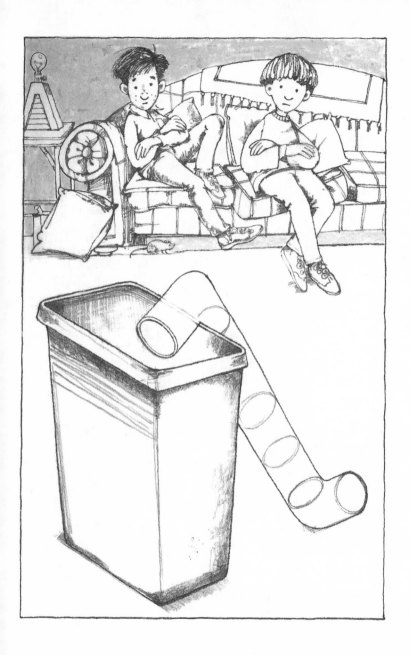

will smell the food and run up the ramp to get it. They'll fall into the wastebasket and then be unable to get out. Then I'll put them in their tank, where they'll be safe and get plenty to eat."

Andy sat on the couch, folded his arms, watched the wastebasket, and waited. Bruce sat next to Andy, folded his arms, and watched and waited, too.

Chapter 7
She's My Friend

Andy stared at the wastebasket. Bruce looked at him, and waited to hear more about his gerbil-catching plan, but Andy was quiet.

"Do you think this will work?" Bruce asked.

"Of course," Andy answered without even turning to face his friend. "Why do you think I did it?"

Bruce was quiet for a minute. Then he asked, "How long do you think it will take?"

"I don't know," Andy answered, clearly impatient with Bruce's questions.

Bruce looked across the room at the ramp, the wastebasket, and the bookcase filled with books and toys. He knew he should be quiet, but he just couldn't be. "What are you thinking?" he asked.

"I'm thinking," Andy answered, again sounding annoyed, "when will you stop asking so many questions?" Then Andy said in a softer tone, "I'm also thinking about Ms. Roman, my mother, and Tamika."

Andy stared straight ahead as he talked. He spoke slowly and softly.

"This year has really been hard for Tamika. First her parents had that accident. Then the Perlmans took her in as a foster child until her parents get better. But now they have to go to South America and she can't go along."

"Why do they have to go there?" Bruce asked.

"They're anthropologists. They study people and they're doing some project for something they're writing."

"Why can't Tamika go?"

"You know she visits her parents every Sunday and she couldn't visit them if she went to South America. And the Perlmans will be moving around a lot. Tamika would have to keep changing schools."

"Oh."

Andy looked at Bruce and said, "You're my good friend."

"I'm your *best* friend," Bruce corrected him.

"Can you keep another secret?" Andy asked.

"I can keep lots of secrets," Bruce answered proudly.

"Well," Andy said, "the agency found a place for Tamika, and the new foster home is not in our district. So she'll have to leave our school. The secret is that I want her to live with us, so she can stay in our class with all her friends." Andy paused for a moment and then added, "Especially me."

"That would be nice," Bruce said. He thought about that for a while. Then he asked, "Would Tamika be your foster sister?"

Andy nodded.

Andy sat very still and stared at the gerbil tunnel for what seemed to Bruce to be a very long time. Tears formed in Andy's eyes as he spoke softly, almost to himself. "With the gerbils loose and Mom pregnant, this is a bad time to ask my parents if Tamika can live here."

Tears rolled down Andy's cheeks. Bruce sat next to him and waited.

"And if Ms. Roman sees Mom at that meeting next week and says something bad about me, my parents will never let Tamika stay, and that's not fair." Andy wiped his cheeks with the back of his hand. "It's not Tamika's fault I wasn't paying attention in class, or the gerbils got loose, or my mom is pregnant."

Bruce turned his wrist slowly and glanced down at his watch. It was four o'clock. He would have to go home in half an hour and they still hadn't done their homework.

"I have to find out soon if Tamika can stay here, before the people at the agency send her to live with that other family." Andy slowly stood, pulled the shirttail out of his pants, wiped his eyes with it, and said, "I'm going to ask Dad now, before something else happens."

"Should I go with you?" Bruce asked.

"No. You stay here and watch for gerbils. I have to do this alone."

Andy went up the basement stairs. He quickly opened then closed the door behind him so no gerbils could get upstairs. He walked past the kitchen and saw that Rachel was back at the table, doing her homework.

"Is Mom better?" Andy asked.

Rachel looked up. "She's a little better. She said I should do my homework." She paused for a moment. Then she said, "Don't worry. I won't tell Mom about the gerbils, and I looked at my autograph book and they didn't chew so much. But you'd better not let them chew up anything else of mine."

"I won't," Andy promised.

Andy went upstairs to look for his father. He looked first in his parents' room. His mother was in bed, with her clothes and shoes still on. Her right arm was folded over her eyes and the barf basin was on the floor next to the bed.

Andy thought, *Dad has a real hard time saying no to me. First I'll get him to say Tamika can stay with us. Then I'll ask Mom and Rachel. Or better yet, he'll ask them.*

Andy looked in his bedroom and Rachel's room for his father, but he didn't find him. Andy went back to the door of his parents' bedroom.

"Hey, Mom, do you know where Dad is?"

Mrs. Russell slowly lifted her left hand and pointed to her closet.

"He's in the closet?"

Mrs. Russell nodded.

Andy opened the door to his mother's closet and looked in. There were racks of his mother's dresses and slacks on either side of the door, with shelves filled with neatly labeled boxes above each of the racks. In the middle of the closet was a rope ladder hanging down from the ceiling. Andy looked up and saw that the hatchway to the attic was open.

Andy climbed the bottom two rungs of the ladder and called, "Are you up there, Dad?"

"Yes."

"I need to talk to you, Dad."

"Come on up."

Andy hated climbing the shaky rope ladder

and going in the cramped, musty attic, but he had to if he was going to ask his father about Tamika. Andy looked up at the open hatchway, held on to the ladder, carefully lifted his right foot onto the first rung and then his left onto the next. He climbed the next three rungs, reached up, held on to the sides of the hatchway, and pulled himself up into the attic.

"Hey, Andy."

Andy leaned over the opening and looked at the ladder as it turned and swung freely. He dreaded having to reach with his foot later to try and find the top rung and make his way back down into his mother's closet. Going down was worse than going up.

Andy turned to his dad, who was crouched in the corner where the sloping roof and bare wood floor met.

"Hey, Dad."

Mr. Russell was holding a pad of paper in a clipboard and one end of a metal tape measure. He pushed the automatic rewind switch and twelve feet of tape raced across the attic floor and into the case. Mr. Russell wrote down some numbers and then told Andy, "I'm thinking of adding

a room up here. With the baby and all, we could use an extra bedroom."

"I need to talk to you, Dad."

"In a minute."

Andy sat on the attic floor and watched his father measure the height of the roof in different parts of the attic. Mr. Russell made chalk marks on the floor and measured the distance from one chalk mark to the next. He wrote some notes. Then he hooked the tape measure to his belt.

Mr. Russell smiled.

"Here's my plan: The stairs will start in the hall and go through Mom's closet. For the windows, I'll break through the roof and build dormers. I'll do it after work and you can help."

"Can we build two bedrooms up here?"

"We don't need two more rooms. We only need one."

"That's why I want to talk to you, Dad." Andy paused. He didn't know what to say.

Mr. Russell walked over and sat on the floor next to Andy. "Is it about the baby?"

Andy shook his head and said, "It's not about the baby."

"The gerbils?"

Andy shook his head. "It's really about Tamika, but first I have to tell you about Ms. Roman."

"This sounds complicated," Mr. Russell said, and smiled.

"Ms. Roman called on me today and I didn't know the answer."

"That's not so terrible, Andy. You can't be expected to know the answer to every question."

"But, Dad, I didn't even know we were doing math. I thought we were doing geography. The answer was some number and I said, 'China.' "

"Oh."

"Dad, I try to listen in class, but she's so boring and she hates me. She only calls on me when I'm thinking about something else."

Andy looked at the floor and said, "I was thinking about Tamika, Dad. Her parents are still in the hospital and the Perlmans have to go to South America."

"Is she going with them?"

"She can't," Andy said slowly. "They'll be moving around a lot and Tamika needs to stay in one place so she can go to school." Andy paused. Then he said softly, "The foster agency found a place for her, but if she lives there she'll have to change schools. If she lives here, she won't have to move anywhere, just next door, and she will stay with me in Ms. Roman's class."

"Here?" Mr. Russell asked. "In this house?"

"She could sleep in Rachel's room, in the extra bed, or when the new room is ready, she could sleep up here."

"We're having a baby. We have no room for someone else."

There were tears in Andy's eyes and they were spilling onto his cheeks. "She's not someone else," Andy said, trying to keep himself from crying. "She's my friend."

Mr. Russell took Andy's hand. He didn't speak for what seemed to Andy to be a long while. Then he said, "Tamika is a nice girl."

Andy nodded.

"And that accident was a real tragedy."

Andy hoped his father was about to say Tamika could live with them. He didn't.

Mr. Russell said, "But what makes you think Rachel would want to share her room? And you see how your mother feels. This is really not a good time for us to have a guest."

"Rachel and Tamika are friends," Andy told his

father. "And Mom's not really sick. She's just pregnant."

Mr. Russell gently held Andy's hand. "I'll speak to your mother," he said, "and I'll speak to Rachel."

"Sure, Dad," Andy said, not hiding his disappointment. He wiped the tears from his cheeks. "You'll ask Mom and Rachel. That's just another way of saying no."

"That's not true at all," Mr. Russell said. "It's a way of saying I can't decide something like this on my own. It wouldn't be fair to the other people who live in this house. I'll speak with your mother, but not until she feels better, and I'll speak to Rachel."

Mr. Russell let go of Andy's hand. They just sat there, quietly, for a while. Then Mr. Russell got up and stood over the hatchway. Before he stepped down he asked, "What about the gerbils? Did you get them all?"

"Yikes!" Andy exclaimed. "I left Bruce in the basement!"

Chapter 8
Lots of Ways to Say No

Mr. Russell started down the ladder.

"And we didn't even begin our home-work," Andy said. "But, I promise, I'll do it all and I'll listen in class, and if Ms. Roman sees Mom at that meeting next week, she'll say how good I am and that I get every answer right."

Mr. Russell reached for Andy. With his father to help him, it was easy going down the rope ladder.

As they stepped out of the closet, Mr. Russell

put his finger to his lips. Mrs. Russell was sleeping.

Andy was careful not to wake her. Before he left the room, he stopped for a moment and looked at his mother. He wondered what she had inside—his brother or his sister?

Then Andy hurried to the basement. He found Bruce there, still sitting on the couch. Bruce's eyes opened wide as soon as Andy closed the door. He stretched out his arms and called across the basement in a loud, excited whisper.

"You should have been here. It was great! A gerbil came out from the toys. It smelled the food. Its nose was twitching like this."

Bruce wrinkled his nose in an effort to show Andy how the gerbil's nose twitched. But he seemed more like someone who was about to sneeze.

"It looked in the wastebasket, then at the tunnel, and then it looked at me. I sat here real still. I didn't want to scare the gerbil. I pretended I was a large stuffed animal."

Bruce held his hands up, signaling the coming triumphant end to his story. "It crawled through the tunnel and fell into the food. I left the gerbil there so you would know I'm not making any of this up."

Andy looked in the wastebasket. A gerbil was in there, happily eating. Andy grabbed its tail and put the gerbil in the middle tank.

"Isn't that great?" Bruce asked.

"Yeah, it's great," Andy answered. "But, we're still missing two, so we'll leave the trap."

Bruce looked at his watch. It was past five.

"I have to go home now. I'm already late for dinner."

"Please," Andy said, "don't go yet. We haven't even started our homework. Call your parents and ask if you can stay here longer. Ask if you can stay for dinner."

Bruce made the call. He spoke to his mother. Then he listened for a while and said, "Sure, Mom," and hung up the telephone.

"My mother said I should remember to thank your parents for dinner," Bruce told Andy, "and that I should be polite."

Andy said, "You're always polite."

"Thank you."

"See that! You even thanked me for saying you're polite."

Andy and Bruce spread their schoolbooks on the floor. Then Andy told Bruce, "My dad said he has to ask Mom and Rachel if Tamika can stay here. That's like saying 'No way!' "

Andy shook his head and said sadly, "Adults have lots of ways to say no."

"Yeah," Bruce said. "My mom's favorite way is 'I'll think about it.' That means no. And 'Maybe later.' That means no, too."

Then Bruce told Andy, "Tamika is real nice. She's good at making friends. She'll be OK."

"I hope you're right," Andy said.

They sat quietly for a while. Then Andy said, "Let's do math first. We'll work separately and compare our answers. If we get the same answers, they're probably right."

Andy and Bruce did the math that way, and the science, too. They were closing their books when Mr. Russell opened the basement door.

"Oh, hi, Bruce. I didn't know you were still here." He looked at the plastic tunnel and the wastebasket and asked, "What's all this?"

Bruce explained about the trap and told Mr. Russell how it had caught a gerbil. He even tried again to twitch his nose like one.

"Oh my," Mr. Russell teased. "When you do that, you look like a gerbil."

"I was just showing you what the gerbil did when it smelled the food."

"Oh," Mr. Russell said. Then he told Andy, "Mom feels better, so we're going to eat now. I made pizza muffins for us and toast for Mom."

Andy told his father, "Bruce's mother already said he can eat with us. Can he, Dad?"

"Sure!" Mr. Russell said. "Put your books away and come upstairs."

Andy and Bruce put their books in their backpacks. Then, as they were going up the basement stairs, Andy told Bruce, "Mom feels good enough to eat toast, so she must be better. At dinner maybe Dad will ask her about Tamika."

Chapter 9
"What?"

Mrs. Russell was sitting by the kitchen table with her legs stretched out, her arms hanging by her sides, and her head resting on the back of the chair. Rachel was sitting next to her, gently patting her mother's hand.

As they came into the kitchen, Bruce whispered to Andy, "Your mother doesn't look so good."

The boys sat down, and Mr. Russell gave each

of them two pizza muffins. The boys ate quietly and watched Mrs. Russell.

She leaned forward and took the piece of toast off her plate. She looked at it. She turned it over and looked at it some more. Then she nibbled on it and sighed.

Mr. Russell leaned forward and asked, "How is it?"

"It's very good."

"Would you like some hot tea?"

Mrs. Russell slowly nodded, "Yes, please," she said. "Herbal tea."

Mr. Russell turned on the burner under the teakettle and took a mug from the shelf above the sink. As he reached for it, he looked up. He paused. Then he turned to Andy and pointed to the ceiling. Mr. Russell had seen the hand-print.

Oh, please, Andy thought, *don't say anything. I don't want Mom to know about it.*

Mrs. Russell was resting her head on the back of her chair again. Rachel was cutting her pizza muffin into bite-size pieces. Neither of them saw Mr. Russell point to himself, then open his hand,

and move it in a circle. Bruce was watching, but Andy didn't care. Bruce was his friend.

Andy shook his head. He didn't know what his father was telling him.

Mr. Russell did it all again. He pointed to himself and moved his open hand in another circle.

Andy still didn't understand.

"He said he'll clean it later," Bruce whispered.

Andy looked at his father. Mr. Russell nodded.

"Clean what?" Rachel asked.

"Nothing," Mr. Russell told her. "I'm just about to make the tea."

He poured boiling water from the kettle into the mug. Then he dipped a tea bag into the water.

Rachel watched her father make the tea. Then she leaned forward and asked her mother, "Would you like some jelly on your toast?"

"Yes, please."

Rachel went to the refrigerator for the jelly.

"Can Tamika live here?" Andy asked quickly.

Mr. Russell dropped the tea bag into the water and frowned at Andy. Rachel turned from the refrigerator.

"What?" Mrs. Russell asked.

"It would only be for a year, until the Perlmans get back from South America. It may even be less, if Tamika's parents get better."

"What?" Mrs. Russell asked again.

"Hey, that wouldn't be fair," Rachel said. "Why can Andy have a friend living here and I can't?"

Andy glared at Rachel "Because *my* friend needs a place to live!" he told her.

"*Your* friend!" Rachel shouted. "Tamika is *my* friend!"

Rachel put the jar of strawberry jelly on the table. Then she said again slowly, "Hey, Tamika *is* my friend, too."

Mrs. Russell put her hands to her ears and said, "Quiet, please!"

Mrs. Russell tapped on her plate with her fork to get her husband's attention and asked, "What's this all about?"

Mr. Russell set the mug of tea on the table, sat next to Mrs. Russell, and explained, "Tamika needs a new place to live. Her parents are still in the hospital and the Perlmans are going away."

"Rachel wants her here," Andy said quickly. "And I want her. And Dad already said she can stay here, so you're the only one left who has to say yes."

"Wait a minute! Wait a minute!" Mr. Russell said. "I never said Tamika can stay here. I said I had to discuss this with your mother."

"Where would she sleep?" Mrs. Russell asked.

Andy said, "She could sleep in the basement."

"With the mice?" Rachel asked.

"They're gerbils," Andy told her.

"Whatever," Rachel said. Then she added, "She can sleep in my room. I have an extra bed."

Mrs. Russell shook her head and said slowly, "But we can't take in someone else now because ..." She looked at Bruce. "Because ...," she said again, and stopped.

Mr. Russell told her, "Bruce knows about the baby."

"He does?"

"Bruce was under Andy's bed when Dad told us you're pregnant," Rachel explained.

Andy looked at his mother. He didn't want her to ask why Bruce was under his bed, so he quickly said, "This all happened when you were barfing. But you look much better now. How do you feel?"

She smiled. "I feel better, thank you. But I do wish you'd be more careful with the words you use. *Barfing* is not a nice word."

Mrs. Russell took a sip of tea and then asked Andy, "Does Tamika know you planned to ask us if she can stay here?"

"Yes, and she really wants to because if she lives with the family the agency found for her, she'll have to change schools. And she might not like her new foster parents, and there are children in that family, and she might not like them, either."

Mrs. Russell shook her head again and said, "You should have asked Dad and me *before* you spoke to Tamika."

Mrs. Russell took another sip of tea. She reached out across the table and patted Andy's hand. She smiled and said, "Of course, we have to tell her she can't live here, but we have to do it gently. Why don't we have her come for dinner tomorrow, so we can explain."

"She's so nice," Andy said. There were tears

88

in his eyes again. "She's my friend," he said, and wiped his eyes. "And she needs us."

"She really is nice," Rachel said.

"I wish we could help her," Mr. Russell said. "Maybe we can help her find some other place to stay."

"I'll ask my friends," Rachel said. "We all like Tamika."

They sat quietly for a while. Finally, Mr. Russell turned to Bruce and said, "Why don't you finish eating and then I'll take you home."

Chapter 10
Pay Attention

Andy stayed up much of the night, wondering what he would tell Tamika. He just *had* to tell her his mother was pregnant. He'd tell her that his mother was sick, barfing all over the place. Maybe then Tamika would understand why she couldn't stay with them.

Then Andy remembered it was a Russell family secret that his mother was going to have a baby. Actually, now it was a Russell-family-and-Bruce secret. Andy didn't know what to do.

The next morning Andy went into the basement to check the wastebasket trap. He found one gerbil in there and put it in the middle tank.

Andy looked at all the gerbils and thought about how crowded they were in the three tanks. The first two gerbils had been fun, but with so many, he was sure they would get him in trouble again. Andy knew he had to find new homes for them. But where? Andy checked the tops of each tank, to be sure the screens were on right. Then he went outside to wait for the bus.

Tamika was late again. She ran up the stairs and into the bus just as Mr. Cole was about to close the door. When she got to the back and sat next to Andy, he knew he should tell her that his parents said she couldn't live with them. But his mother had said *she* would explain. So Andy just told Tamika, "I spoke to my parents last night and they want you to come to dinner."

"Really? That's great! If they want me to come to dinner that means they might want to become my foster parents. Oh, that's so great!"

Andy looked at Tamika. Her happy smile brightened her whole face. Andy didn't know how he could tell her that his parents had invited her to say they *couldn't* be her foster parents.

"Did they say where I'd sleep?" Tamika asked. "I guess I'll be in Rachel's room. Does she mind?"

Andy shook his head. He looked down at the floor of the bus and thought, *Let Mom and Dad tell Tamika why she can't live with us!*

"Did they say when I could move in?" Tamika asked.

"Let's not talk about that now," Andy said, "because...well, just because."

"Sure," Tamika said. "We can talk about it at dinner."

"Sure," Andy mumbled. He was glad Bruce was sitting far enough away not to hear the conversation.

When the bus got to school, Andy, Tamika, and Bruce hurried to their classroom. Ms. Roman was standing by the door. She smiled at Andy and said, "Do you remember what you promised? You said today you would pay attention in class."

"Yes, I did," Andy told her, "and I will. I really will."

Andy sat in his seat and wondered how he could possibly listen to Ms. Roman all day. He was sure she was the worst teacher ever. She was surely the most boring teacher he had ever had. He watched her go to the chair by her desk and sit down. Andy knew what was coming. She would check the attendance and then start talking. She would talk on and on.

How can I stay awake? Andy asked himself.

He bent down and retied his sneakers. He tied them really tight, so his feet were uncomfortable. He tightened his belt, too. *Good,* he thought, *maybe my aching feet and stomach will keep me focused on Ms. Boring Roman.* Next, Andy wrote on the cover of his notebook PAY ATTENTION! and WAKE UP! in large block letters.

All during class he tried to listen to Ms. Roman explain about multiplication, but he kept thinking about Tamika instead. In the middle of the math lesson, Ms. Roman looked at Andy. She smiled, so Andy did, too.

"Well, Andrew, what's the answer?"

Andy looked at the chalkboard. It was covered with numbers. He looked down at his notebook, pretending to be checking his work. "Five hundred and fourteen?" Andy said.

"I know! I know!" Stacy Ann Jackson called out.

"Yes, Stacy Ann," Ms. Roman said.

"Sixteen thousand, nine hundred."

"That's right."

Well, Andy thought, *at least I answered with a number and not the name of a country.*

As soon as Ms. Roman turned to write something on the chalkboard, Stacy Ann smiled and whispered to Andy, "*I* pay attention in class and *I* do my work."

Andy thought of lots of things to answer Stacy Ann, but he didn't want to get into more trouble with Ms. Roman, so he just stuck out his tongue.

Andy was relieved when Ms. Roman announced it was time for lunch. It was difficult to pretend for so long to be a good, attentive student.

Before he left the classroom, Andy loosened his belt and his sneaker laces. In the cafeteria he sat with Tamika and Bruce. Bruce opened his lunch bag and took out a sandwich, two containers of orange juice, a bag of cookies, and an

apple. He shook his head and sighed, "My mom never gives me enough."

"Here," Andy told him. He took a small bag of pretzels from his lunch bag and gave the rest to Bruce. "Have a party."

As Tamika unwrapped her sandwich, she told Andy, "I think I'll wear my fancy dress tonight."

Andy pushed a straw into the chocolate milk container, and as he took a sip he said, "That's nice."

Bruce was busy eating. Andy was glad he didn't tell Tamika that she couldn't live with the Russells. *He really is good at keeping secrets,* Andy thought.

When they returned to class, Ms. Roman told Andy, "You were really very good this morning. I was pleased."

Andy wanted Ms. Roman to still be pleased at the end of the day. When he got to his seat, he sat down and took off his left sneaker. He broke the eraser off his pencil and dropped it in his sneaker. Then he put the shoe on and tied it. He put his left foot down. *Good,* Andy thought. *It hurts. Now, any time I start to daydream, I'll stomp my foot. That should wake me.*

Andy stomped his left foot twice during the geography lesson and three more times during science. Just before dismissal, Ms. Roman talked about the school carnival. Andy didn't have to stomp his foot then. He thought working on a carnival for charity was exciting. Ms. Roman still wanted suggestions for fun booths, as well as donations of old books and toys for prizes.

Bruce raised his hand and said, "I have some toy cars I don't use anymore. I can give you those."

"That would be nice," Ms. Roman said.

Andy thought that winning Bruce's old broken toy cars would be more like losing. Some of them had no wheels. He remembered the carnival he had gone to at the firehouse. He had tried to toss Ping-Pong balls into little goldfish bowls. If he'd got one in, he would have won a goldfish. Now, that's a prize!

"And I can bring in some books I no longer read," Stacy Ann Jackson said.

Suddenly Andy had a great idea.

"We can give away gerbils," Andy called out. "They're great pets. A gerbil is an even better prize than a goldfish because they go through mazes and have babies. What do you think, Ms. Roman? I can bring in lots of them."

Ms. Roman smiled. "That's a good idea," she said.

Andy was standing now. "Whoever wins one will just have to promise to take care of his gerbil and to love it. That's all I ask," he said.

Ms. Roman was excited by Andy's idea. "If your parents agree to give up some of your gerbils, I think we have our prizes."

"Oh, my parents will say yes," Andy said. "I'm sure of that."

When they got on the bus, Bruce asked Andy if he would give him a gerbil. "I'm not sure I'll be able to win one."

"Sure," Andy told Bruce. "If I give away the rest of them as prizes, I can even let you have one of the tanks."

Tamika told Andy, "Giving the gerbils as prizes is a great idea." She smiled. "It's brilliant, Andy. Simply brilliant."

Bruce wasn't coming to Andy's house, so he got off at his regular stop. Andy, Tamika, Rachel, and the Belmonts got off at the next stop.

Tamika told Andy, "I decided I *will* wear my

flower dress for dinner. It's my best one. My mom bought it for me just before the accident."

After they crossed the street, she said to Andy, "I'll see you at about five." Then she told Rachel, "And I'll see you, too."

"I don't know why she's so happy," Rachel said. "Doesn't she know Dad is making dinner, so it'll be pizza muffins again or his yucky meat loaf. The last time the meat was raw and I found a shirt button in my piece."

Andy told his sister, "She thinks Mom and Dad will tell her she can move in with us."

"Oh," Rachel said.

Andy watched Tamika go into the house next door. He didn't care what was for dinner. He just hoped Tamika's new foster family would be as nice to her as the Perlmans had been.

Chapter 11
We Have to Talk

Rachel unlocked the front door and went straight to the kitchen. She opened her backpack, took out her schoolbooks, and put them on the table. Then she sat down to do her homework.

Andy dropped his backpack on the floor by the front door and went downstairs to check his gerbil trap. He found one gerbil in there. He put it in the middle tank.

That should be all of them, he thought. Andy

counted seven gerbils, but he wasn't sure if there were six and he had counted one twice, or if there were really seven. He counted again. Seven. He had them all.

Andy took the long tunnel apart and put pieces back into each of the tanks. He knew he should reassemble them into the twisted tunnels the gerbils loved, but he didn't have time. He had to prepare for Tamika's visit.

Andy went to the kitchen.

"You have to go somewhere else. I have to set the table," he told Rachel. "Tamika is coming."

"Andy," Rachel said. "You're making too much of this dinner. Mom and Dad already decided Tamika can't live here. And anyway, I do my homework in the kitchen. If you want to set the table, do it in the dining room."

Andy decided not to argue with Rachel. Tamika was "company," so they would eat in the dining room. He would set the table real fancy, like the time Mom's boss, Mr. Kamen, the principal of the high school, came.

Andy opened the cupboard and took out five place mats, five fancy dinner plates, and five salad plates. He got flatware from the drawer, napkins, and the salt and pepper shakers. He set everything on the dining-room table, then cut out five paper squares, folded them, and made place cards. Andy wrote MOM, DAD, ANDY, RACHEL, and TAMIKA on the cards, one name to a card. Beside each name, even Rachel's, he drew a large red heart. He set each card on a plate. He put Tamika's plate next to his.

Andy checked to be sure everything was right. Dinner plates, salad plates, napkins, knives, forks, spoons. He looked at the table for a while and it seemed to him something was missing, but he didn't know what.

Andy sat in his seat and imagined he was eating spaghetti. He pretended to sprinkle on some pepper. Then he reached for his fork, dug into the mound of imaginary spaghetti, and twirled it around. One strand was dangling. It just wouldn't stay with the others, so Andy took the knife and cut it. Then Andy opened his mouth wide and pretended to eat.

Andy chewed for a while. Then he looked across the table to one of the empty chairs and asked, "What are you pointing at, Mom?" He looked down at his shirt and said, "Yikes! Tomato sauce!" He reached for his napkin and wiped it across his shirt.

Andy imagined he'd finished eating the entire mound of spaghetti. He put the fork and knife down, and just as he started to reach across his dinner plate for something to drink, he realized what was missing. Glasses.

Andy got up, went to the kitchen, and took the fancy glasses from the cabinet, the ones with the large $\mathscr{R}$ etched in the middle. He was putting them out when the front door opened. Andy's parents were home. Mrs. Russell looked tired as she walked toward the stairs.

"Hi, Mom!" called Rachel as her mother passed the kitchen.

"Hello," she answered in a faint voice.

Mrs. Russell looked in the dining room. She watched Andy put out the glasses. Then she asked, "What are you doing? Why did you take out our best glasses and dishes? And why aren't we eating in the kitchen?"

"Did you forget, Mom? Tamika is coming for dinner."

"Oh yes, how could I forget?" Mrs. Russell asked. "I wish I could prepare the meal, but I'm too tired to cook and I'm still a little nauseous. Your father will make dinner. I hope you told Tamika not to expect anything special."

Rachel was standing by the kitchen door. "Why should Andy say that?" she asked. "We'll prepare a feast."

"Just don't make a mess," Mrs. Russell said, and then started upstairs.

"Wait! Wait, Mom," Andy said suddenly. "I just remembered. I have some great news, great for you, at least. I may be giving my gerbils away as prizes at my school's charity carnival."

Mrs. Russell stopped and looked at Andy. Then she smiled and said, "That *is* great news. Whenever I think of all those gerbils living in the basement, I have this terrible fear that one day they might get out and be all over the house."

"Do you, Mom?" Rachel asked. "I get nightmares about that. I imagine gerbils everywhere, even under our beds, with Andy and his friends crawling after them. *Ooh!*" Rachel shook her shoulders as if she was horrified.

Andy glared at Rachel. Then he told his mother, "If I give them away at the carnival, we won't have to worry about that."

Mrs. Russell smiled and went slowly upstairs.

Mr. Russell handed Andy a box from the bakery and said, "Here's the dessert. Please put this in the kitchen." Then he looked in the dining room and said, "Well, I see the table is set. Who wants to help me cook? I'm making my surprise meat loaf."

Andy said, "I'll help, Dad. I'll make sure you cook the meat long enough."

"And I'll make the salad," Rachel said.

Andy, Rachel, and Mr. Russell went into the kitchen.

"What's the surprise?" Andy asked.

"You'll see."

Mr. Russell opened a cookbook to the meatloaf page and put it on the counter near Andy, along with a metal loaf pan and a mixing bowl, a package of chopped beef, a raw egg, an onion, a box of bread crumbs, a can of tomato sauce, salt and pepper, a knife, and a measuring cup.

Andy emptied the package of chopped meat into the bowl. He squeezed the meat and smiled as it oozed through his fingers. It reminded him of making mud pies when he had been much younger. It had been fun making the pies, even though nobody would eat them. Andy rolled the meat into three balls and made a snowman, a *meat*man!

"What are you doing?" his father asked.

Andy answered, "I'm mixing the meat."

"What are you mixing it with?"

"My hands." Andy held up his two meat-covered hands.

"Yuck!" Rachel said. She was cutting a tomato into perfect wedges and carefully putting them into a wooden bowl.

"I meant," Mr. Russell said slowly, "are you mixing the meat with the egg and onion and other ingredients or are you just playing?"

Rachel answered, "He's just playing."

"I asked Andy," Mr. Russell said.

"I was just playing," Andy said. He shook the beef off his hands and into the bowl. Then he washed his hands in the sink.

Mr. Russell beat the egg, chopped the onion, and added them to the meat. He poured in bread crumbs and the can of tomato sauce, then tossed in a pinch of salt and pepper. Andy mixed it all together with his hands.

While Andy dumped the mixture into the loaf

pan and pressed it into shape, Mr. Russell worked on his surprise—two hard-boiled eggs that he set deep in the center of the meat loaf. "It'll look nice when I cut a slice and inside is a circle of yellow yolk surrounded by a circle of egg white."

Andy said, "I think one of the stacking clowns in the middle would be a better surprise, or I could write lots of little fortunes and stick them in there. Instead of fortune cookies, we would have fortune meat loaf. I'll write things like 'A tall handsome stranger will do your homework' and 'You will sit on a frog and be hoppy' and 'You will find a new home with friends.'"

Mr. Russell said, "Eggs are a good surprise," and he put the meat loaf in the oven.

He and Andy were preparing corn and potatoes when Tamika arrived. She was wearing her pretty flower-print dress and had a red ribbon in her hair. She gave Mr. Russell a bouquet of flowers and a large, covered plastic bowl, and said, "Thank you for inviting me."

Rachel was standing in the doorway to the kitchen. She was holding the wooden bowl with the salad she had made.

"These flowers are beautiful," Mr. Russell said.

"Mrs. Perlman told me to pick them for you," Tamika said. "They're from her yard."

"What's in the bowl?" Andy asked.

"I made salad for everyone."

Rachel held up the wooden bowl and said, "So did I."

Mr. Russell looked at Rachel, then at Tamika. "Why don't you mix them together," he suggested.

The two girls looked at each other for a moment. Then they smiled. Tamika poured her salad into the wooden bowl. Rachel tossed the two salads together.

Andy looked in the bowl and told Tamika, "I can tell which tomatoes Rachel cut and which are yours. Rachel's are all the same. Yours are all different sizes."

"I like diversity," Tamika said.

"What?" Andy asked.

Tamika explained, "I like it when things are not all the same."

Mr. Russell put the flowers in a vase and set it in the middle of the dining-room table.

RRRR!

The timer rang. Mr. Russell said, "Excuse me," went into the kitchen, and turned off the oven. He put on large cloth mitts, took out the meat loaf, and told Andy, Rachel, and Tamika, "Why don't you go to the bathroom and wash your hands and then sit down while I get Mom."

Andy said to Tamika, "I helped make the meat loaf." He showed her a trace of raw beef caught beneath his fingernails. "Chopped-up, mushed-up cow," he told her just before he washed it out.

"It's fun squeezing chopped meat with your hands, isn't it?" Tamika asked.

"Yeah," Andy said as he washed his hands. He shook off the water, went into the dining room, and sat down. Rachel and Tamika washed and dried their hands. They, too, entered the dining room. Rachel sat, but Tamika stood behind her chair.

"Why don't you sit?" Rachel asked.

"I'm waiting for the host and hostess."

"Are you talking about my parents?" Andy asked.

Tamika nodded.

Andy and Rachel got up and waited, too, with their hands on the back of their chairs. When

Mr. and Mrs. Russell entered the dining room, Mrs. Russell looked at Andy, Rachel, and Tamika for a moment. Then she smiled and said, "Hello, Tamika. How are you?"

"I'm just fine, Mrs. Russell."

"Are you standing to be polite?" Mrs. Russell asked.

"Yes," Tamika answered.

"How nice." Mrs. Russell pulled out her chair and sat down.

"I'm not standing to be polite," Andy explained as he and Rachel pulled out their chairs and sat down, too. "I was standing because she was."

Mrs. Russell noticed the flowers. "Oh, Charles, that was so sweet. I love flowers."

Andy said, "Tamika brought them and some of the salad, too. She mixed her salad with the one Rachel made."

"Oh my, that wasn't at all necessary, but very much appreciated." Mrs. Russell smiled. "I wish my children would learn to be such polite and thoughtful guests."

"See, Mom," Andy said. "Tamika can teach us lots of good stuff."

"Do you really think so?" Tamika asked.

Mr. Russell clapped his hands and said, "Let's eat!"

Rachel and Tamika served the salad on the small plates. Mrs. Russell said it was delicious.

"At my house," Tamika said, "we used to take turns making supper. Mom and Dad made real food, but I kept making the same thing—peanut butter sandwiches. Mom was tired of eating sandwiches, so she taught me to make salads. When I put some tuna in the salad, it's a whole meal."

"I love tuna in a salad," Mrs. Russell said. "It's delicious, and taking turns preparing meals is a great idea. Maybe we should do that."

"And whoever made the meal at my house cleaned the pots and dishes. That's one reason I make sandwiches and salads. There's very little mess."

"Well," Mr. Russell said as he got up, "who's ready for my surprise meat loaf?"

"I know the surprise," Andy said.

Mr. Russell brought in a bowl of corn and a large platter with the meat loaf surrounded by baby potatoes. He cut a slice of meat loaf and held it up for everyone to see. "Surprise!" he called out when they all saw the egg in the middle.

"That's so pretty," Tamika said.

Mr. Russell gave Rachel, Andy, and Tamika a slice. Rachel leaned really close and looked at the meat on her plate. "And so cooked," she said.

Mrs. Russell only ate potatoes. When she finished them, she asked Tamika, "How are your parents?"

"They're getting better, but very slowly. I don't know when they'll get to go home."

Mr. Russell leaned forward and said, "We know you'd like to stay here for a while, but . . ."

Mrs. Russell interrupted her husband. "But we still have to talk about it."

Andy looked at his mother. He wondered what there was to talk about. She had already decided she and his dad couldn't be Tamika's foster parents.

"Well, if we have to talk about it, we'll talk," Mr. Russell said. "Meanwhile, I'll clear the table and we can have the apple pie I brought home for dessert."

Tamika took her plate and Andy's, got up, and said, "I'll help."

"No," Mr. Russell said, and took the plates from her. "You just sit. You're our guest. Andy and Rachel will help."

Chapter 12
The Andersons

After dessert everyone helped clean up. Then Tamika thanked the Russells again for inviting her. "And thank you for the delicious meal," she said. As Andy walked with her to the door, she whispered to him, "Your mother said she has to think about letting me live here. I think that means yes."

"It could also mean no," Andy whispered. "When parents say they have to think about something, that's what it usually means."

"I hope you're wrong," Tamika said. Then she said, "Good-bye," and left.

Andy returned to the kitchen to talk to his parents, but only Rachel was there. She was eating the leftover apple pie.

"Where are Mom and Dad?" Andy asked.

Rachel's mouth was filled with pie. She pointed with her fork to the ceiling. Andy looked up and saw his handprint there. He hoped his father would get it off before his mother noticed it.

"Where are they?" Andy asked again.

"In their room," Rachel said with her mouth still full of pie.

Andy hurried up the stairs. The door to his parents' bedroom was closed, but he could hear them talking. He tiptoed to the door and listened.

"She's such a nice girl," his mother said. "And I don't think she'll be any trouble. Both Rachel and Andy like her. I expect Rachel and Andy to help with the baby. Maybe Tamika would help, too."

"I'm sure she would," Mr. Russell said.

"And Tamika is so polite. Andy is right. Maybe she'll teach him and Rachel 'good stuff.'"

Andy put his ear against the door.

"And," Mrs. Russell continued, "I know I said this before, but she really is such a nice girl. I think I'd like having her live here."

Andy's parents were quiet for a while. *Maybe they're reading,* Andy thought, *or getting undressed.* Andy waited by the door. Then he heard his father say, "I don't think we can simply decide to take her in. We have to be sure she still wants to stay here. And the foster agency probably has to approve us."

"Maybe we can take turns making dinner," Mrs. Russell said. "That's what Tamika and her parents used to do. With her, there would be five of us, so each of us would prepare dinner just once every five days." Then she said, "I do think Tamika would be a good influence on Rachel and Andy."

Mr. Russell asked, "Are you sure you want this extra responsibility, especially now?"

"Yes, I'm sure."

"Then we have to talk with Rachel and Andy. First we have to be sure Rachel is willing to share her room. And we have to ask Andy if he still wants Tamika to live here."

Andy heard his father get up from the bed. He

ran to his room. He had just reached it when he heard his parents' bedroom door open.

"Rachel! Rachel!" Mr. Russell called.

"Coming, Dad!" she called up the stairs.

Andy watched his sister go into his parents' bedroom and close the door. He imagined his sister saying, "What if she snores? What then?" But then he realized Rachel liked Tamika as much as he did.

His parents' bedroom door opened and Mr. Russell said, "Andy, could you please come in here."

Andy walked slowly into their room. He looked at his mother. She was sitting on their bed, propped up with pillows. She was smiling.

"Andy," Mrs. Russell said, "your father, Rachel, and I have talked it over, and until Tamika's parents get better—or until the Perlmans return from South America—we would like to be her foster family."

"You would? Really?"

"And," Mr. Russell said, "Rachel said Tamika could stay in her room."

"Can I call her? Can I tell her?" Andy asked.

"Yes, you may," Mrs. Russell said. "And I'd like to speak with her, too."

Andy called Tamika from his parents' room. "They said *yes!*" Andy shouted into the telephone. "Oh, I'm sorry for screaming, Mrs. Perlman," he said softly. "This is Andy. Can I please speak with Tamika."

Hurry, please, hurry, Andy thought.

Andy waited.

Oh, what's taking you so long? Andy wondered.

"Tamika, Tamika!" Andy said when she finally got on the telephone. "I have some good news. No, the *best* news. The best news ever."

Andy told Tamika she could live with his family.

"Oh, this is so great!" Tamika cried. "I don't want to change schools. I don't want to live in someone's house who I don't even know. I'm so happy." Then she asked, "Are you sure your parents said I could live with you?" But she didn't wait for Andy to answer. "And the Perlmans were worried about what would happen to their house while they're away. Now I can watch it for them. I can water their plants and feed their fish. And we can do homework together every night! Oh, this is so great!"

"May I talk to her?" Andy's mother asked.

When Mrs. Russell took the telephone, Tamika told her, "Oh, thank you. Thank you so much."

"You don't have to thank me," Mrs. Russell said. "We haven't done anything yet, and I know it will be our pleasure to have you here. But there are a lot of arrangements to be made first. May I talk to Mrs. Perlman?"

Mrs. Russell and Mrs. Perlman talked about the foster agency. Mrs. Perlman said she would talk with the people at the agency and that Mr. Rutledge, Tamika's caseworker, would probably call to meet the Russells.

Ding! Ding!

The front doorbell rang.

Andy's mother was still talking to Mrs. Perlman on the phone. She waved to Andy, gesturing for him to see who was at the door.

Andy ran downstairs. He pushed open the mail slot, looked through it, and saw Tamika's knees. Andy quickly opened the door and they hugged.

"This is so great!" Tamika said. "But there's just one thing."

"I know," Andy told her. "The agency."

"No, not that. That's not a problem. Someone from the agency will come here to talk to your family. No, that's not it."

Andy waited.

Suddenly Tamika didn't seem so excited.

"What is it?" Andy asked.

Tamika took a small step back. She was looking down. "It's my parents," she said softly. "I want them to meet you and your family before we do anything, before I move in—even before we talk to the agency."

"Sure," Andy said.

"You see, I've told them about you, but just that you're my friend. If I'm going to live here, they have to meet you and your parents."

"Sure," Andy said again.

"Maybe we can go tomorrow, after school."

"Yeah, sure. I'll ask my parents."

Tamika waited by the door while Andy went upstairs.

Mrs. Russell was in bed. Her eyes were closed. Andy leaned real close to see if she was sleeping.

"Mom," Andy whispered.

She didn't respond.

Andy got even closer. Their noses almost touched. "Mom," he whispered again.

Mrs. Russell opened her eyes. "Oh my," she said. "What are you doing?"

"I was just seeing if you're sleeping," Andy said. "I have to ask you something."

"I *was* resting," Mrs. Russell said. "Now, what's your question?"

"Where's Dad? I have to ask him, too."

Mrs. Russell rubbed her eyes and said, "He's in the attic."

Andy went into the closet. The rope ladder was hanging down from the open hatchway in the ceiling.

"Dad," Andy called up toward the hatchway, "I have to ask you and Mom something."

Mr. Russell came to the hatchway and looked down at Andy. "What is it?"

Andy stood at the door to the closet. He looked from his mother, who was sitting up in her bed, to his father in the attic. "Tamika is real happy about living here, but before she moves in, her parents have to meet us. Can we go see them tomorrow?"

"I can be home by four tomorrow afternoon," Mr. Russell said. "We can go then."

"And we'll take Rachel," Mrs. Russell added.

Andy hurried downstairs to tell Tamika.

"That's good," she said, "and *please,* don't tell anyone at school about this until we're sure. Don't even tell Bruce."

The next day in school, Andy had to stop and think before he spoke. He could talk to Tamika about their secret, but not about his mom being pregnant. And he could talk to Bruce about that, but not about Tamika. This was a lot for Andy to keep track of. He was glad the gerbils were all back in their tanks and he didn't have to worry about keeping that secret anymore.

He paid attention in class and even answered a math problem correctly. When he did, Stacy Ann Jackson turned to face him and said, "Lucky guess." But Andy knew he wasn't just lucky. If only he could pay attention in class, he would be a good student. If only Ms. Roman wasn't so boring.

Tamika went to the Russells' house after school, and at four o'clock they all went to the rehabilitation center to visit with Tamika's parents.

It was a short drive to the center. Mr. Russell parked the car and everyone followed Tamika to the front entrance. They all signed the visitors' book and the man at the front desk gave them each a visitor's pass to clip on their shirts. Andy and his parents and Rachel followed Tamika into the elevator.

"This place smells funny," Andy whispered, but no one responded.

As they got off on the third floor, a nurse wheeled an old man into the elevator. The man's head was resting on his shoulder.

Tamika gently touched his hand and said, "Hello, Mr. Fischer."

He smiled.

While the nurse kept her foot by the elevator door to keep it from closing, she told Tamika, "Your parents are in the solarium."

"Thank you," Tamika said, and went to the left, leading the Russells down a long hallway lined with doors. The place was quiet and warm, and Andy felt uncomfortable there.

The first door they passed was open. Andy looked in and saw an old woman, with long white hair, sitting in a wheelchair and looking up at a television mounted on the wall. The woman was wearing a robe and slippers. Andy felt he shouldn't be looking at the woman in her robe, so he quickly turned away, and when they passed other open doors in the hall, Andy was careful not to look in.

The Russells followed Tamika to a room with large windows. People were sitting in front of a large television set. There was a game show on and the host was shouting about some prize, but most of the seated people didn't seem to be paying any attention to him. Tamika walked past them to two people who were sitting by one of the large windows, with their backs to the television.

Mr. Russell whispered, "They must be Tamika's parents."

The Russells stood quietly and waited until Tamika signaled for them to come over. Andy didn't know why his parents and Rachel walked forward so slowly, but he knew why he did: He was a little scared. He wondered what people looked like after a really bad car accident.

"You have to stand here," Tamika said, pointing directly in front of her parents. "It's hard for them to turn."

Andy walked to a spot in front of the two

125

wheelchairs. He was looking down, so the first he saw of the Andersons was their feet, resting on small square metal plates attached to each chair. Andy looked up a little and saw their hands. Their feet and hands looked fine to Andy, until he realized they didn't move. Then Andy looked up and saw their faces, bent slightly forward. They looked like regular people to Andy, regular people who stayed very still.

"Mom, Dad," Tamika said. "These are my friends, Andy and Rachel."

"Hello," Andy said. He started to step forward and reach out to shake Mr. Anderson's hand, but he quickly pulled his hand back.

Rachel smiled. She slowly lifted her right hand and waved it a little.

Mr. Anderson mumbled something.

"Dad said, 'Hello,'" Tamika explained.

"And these are Mr. and Mrs. Russell," Tamika said.

"You have a wonderful daughter," Mrs. Russell said. "You must be very proud of her."

Tamika's mom and dad smiled. Mr. Anderson mumbled something.

"My dad said, 'Thank you,'" Tamika explained.

"We hope Tamika can stay with us for a while," Mrs. Russell said. "She'll stay in Rachel's room. We have an extra bed there."

The Andersons smiled again. Andy assumed their smiles meant, "Yes, she *can* stay with you."

Mrs. Anderson said, "We think Tamika is the sweetest girl in the world and you have all been the nicest friends to her."

She spoke a lot more clearly than Mr. Anderson. Andy understood her easily.

"Tamika talks about you all the time," Mrs. Anderson continued. "She loves you all, and if she loves you, so do we."

Tamika blushed.

There were tears in Andy's eyes when Mrs. Anderson said Tamika loved him and his family.

Mrs. Russell patted Mrs. Anderson's hand. Mr. Russell just smiled.

Andy and his parents and Rachel stood there for another couple of minutes, until Mrs. Russell said, "Tamika, we'll wait for you by the elevator."

"You visit as long as you want," Mr. Russell

said, turning to walk away. "We don't mind waiting."

As Andy walked through the hall of the rehabilitation center, he thought about the escaped gerbils, Rachel's chewed-up autograph book, and his problems with Ms. Roman, and he realized those weren't *real* troubles. At least his parents were healthy and he didn't have to live in someone else's house.

When they were all downstairs, Tamika said in a determined voice that Andy hadn't heard before, "My parents look *very* good and they're getting better. It's just taking a long time."

Tamika stopped, turned to face Andy, and said, "It's so good I have friends like you, your family, and the Perlmans."

Tamika smiled and that made Andy feel better.

In the car everyone discussed having Tamika move in. They made all kinds of plans: where she would hang her clothes, where she and Andy would do their homework, how they would make her a real—though temporary—member of the family. Mrs. Russell asked her what she liked to eat for breakfast. Everyone seemed really happy.

Early the next week, Mr. Rutledge came from

the agency and looked at the room Tamika would share with Rachel. Then he sat by the kitchen table. Andy and Rachel waited in the living room while Mr. Rutledge spoke with Mr. and Mrs. Russell. Soon the Russells joined Andy in the living room and told Rachel to go talk with Mr. Rutledge in the kitchen.

"Did he have lots of questions?" Andy asked. "Is he nice? Did he say Tamika can live here?"

"Don't worry so much," Mr. Russell said.

But Andy *did* worry.

Rachel came out of the kitchen. She was smiling. "Your turn," she said to Andy.

Mr. Rutledge was writing in a large folder. Andy stood by the entrance to the kitchen and waited. Mr. Rutledge stopped writing. Then he turned and saw Andy standing there.

"Come in," Mr. Rutledge said. "Sit down."

Andy sat in his regular place at the table.

"So you're Andy Russell," Mr. Rutledge said, and smiled.

"Is that good?" Andy asked.

"Yes. Yes," Mr. Rutledge assured Andy. "It's very good. Tamika has told me some very nice things about you."

"Really?"

"Yes, really," Mr. Rutledge answered.

"Now," Mr. Rutledge continued, "are you aware that Tamika would not simply be coming for a visit? She would be living here."

"Yes," Andy answered. "That would be *so* great."

"When Tamika is here," Mr. Rutledge went on, "you would have two sisters, not just one."

Andy smiled.

Then Mr. Rutledge asked, "Do you and Rachel get along?"

Andy looked down at the table and said softly, "Sometimes we argue."

"Do you hit each other?" Mr. Rutledge asked.

"No," Andy said. "We just argue."

Mr. Rutledge smiled. "All siblings argue," he said. "That's normal."

Mr. Rutledge wrote in his folder. He looked up for a moment and Andy expected him to say something. But he just smiled to himself, looked down again, and wrote some more.

Andy didn't know what to do. He felt uncomfortable watching Mr. Rutledge write, but he didn't think he should just leave the kitchen.

Maybe, he thought, *he has something else to ask me.*

Andy sat there for a while, but there were no more questions. Then Mr. Rutledge closed the folder and called Andy's parents and Rachel into the kitchen.

"Of course," he told them, "I will recommend that your home be approved by the agency. And I'm sure Tamika will be very happy here."

The Russells thanked him and walked with him to the door.

Andy waited for the door to close. He looked through the mail slot and watched Mr. Rutledge get into his car. Then, when he was sure Mr. Rutledge could not hear him, Andy stretched out his arms and shouted, "YAHOO!" He hugged his parents. He even hugged Rachel.

"This is good news," Mr. Russell said.

"But it won't be easy for Tamika," Mrs. Russell cautioned. "We have to make her feel comfortable here, that we're her family."

Andy wasn't worried about that.

That night, before Andy fell asleep, he thought about the future. Tamika would be living in his house and that would be great. He thought about the school carnival. That would be fun. And if he gave away all of his gerbils, maybe he could get some other animals to put in the tanks—maybe chameleons or a gecko. Then Andy thought about his mother and the new baby. *It wouldn't be so bad if it turned out to be a girl. Maybe the girl will grow up to be like Tamika. That would be OK. Or maybe it will be a boy, a boy like me. That would be OK, too.*

Turn the page for a sneak peek
at Andy's next adventure. . . .

So, now it's settled that Tamika is moving in with the Russells. All of Andy's gerbils are safely back in their cages. Ms. Roman didn't call his parents after all. And Andy didn't tell one secret to someone he shouldn't have.

His troubles are over, right?

WRONG.

Read *Andy and Tamika* to find out just how much trouble Andy (and his gerbils) can get into at school. If Stacy Ann Jackson has anything to say about it, Andy will face more messes than he can handle.

And what about the baby—will it be a boy or a girl? Andy isn't the only one dying to find out.

Join Andy in all of his adventures! If you liked
The Many Troubles of Andy Russell, you'll enjoy reading
the other books in this exciting new series about Andy,
his friends, and his never-ending escapades.